WHAT IS NADI ASTROLOGY?

Its rules and working principles

Yayathi

"वक्रतुण्ड महाकाय सुर्यकोटि समप्रभ
निर्विघ्नं कुरु मे देव सर्वकार्येषु सर्वदा"

CONTENTS

PREFACE

I am pleased to present this book based on Nadi Astrology before you. Nadi Astrology is regarded as the most ancient form of Astrology that had been practiced thousands of years ago, even before Sage Parashara wrote Brihat Parashara Hora Shastra! Many often imply that Nadi Astrology is not of human origin. According to some sources, Shiva Nadi is the oldest form of Nadi Astrology because it's said to have originated from a conversation between Lord Shiva and his concert, Goddess Parvathi.

When we think about Nadi Astrology, the first thing that comes to our mind is a bundle of palm leaves inscribed with millions of birth charts and predictions. It is said that the birth charts of every single person born into this world, including those yet to be born, are recorded in those manuscripts. It's hard to believe that the birth charts of every single person living in this world are recorded somewhere, let alone of the ones that are not yet born! I am sure you would agree that it would require some serious supernatural abilities to achieve this remarkable feat. Coming back to the present moment, it goes without saying that the chances for you to find your birth chart among those manuscripts are slim to none owing to the sheer population numbers alone.

Still, the sages must have undertaken this gargantuan task of casting millions of birth charts in those manuscripts because they believed that at least some of their descendants would study the methods of divination used in those texts, and thereby, their efforts would prove helpful to mankind. People like Shri R.G Rao must have realized this, and it's quite evident from the sheer amount of time and effort he had put into studying those manuscripts and decoding the methods of predictions used in Nadi Astrology.

There are different types of Nadis, Shiva Nadi, Brahma Nadi, Muruga Nadi, Atri Nadi, Shakti Nadi, Ganesh Nadi, Nandi Nadi, Bhrigu Nadi, Jeeva Nadi, Drava Nadi, Suka Nadi, Agasthyar Nadi, Bogar Nadi, Chandra Kala Nadi are some of them. This book covers the rules and working principles of Nadi Astrology to be adhered to while predicting results. This work is based on Bhrigu Nandi Nadi, introduced by Late Shri R.G Rao, who spent most of his life researching the subject, and also includes the facts that I have found from my research. I request the readers to forgive any mistakes made in this book kindly. I want to thank my Parents, Gurus, and God for their invaluable support.

Om Vigneswaraya Namah

May Lord Ganesha, the remover of all obstacles, shower his blessings upon us all.

Om Namah Shivaya

May the Supreme Power, Lord Shiva Shower His blessings upon us all.

WHAT IS BHRIGU NANDI NADI?

Bhrigu Nandi Nadi is a system of Nadi Astrology introduced by Late Shri R.G Rao from the light of his research on Bhrigu Nadi and Nandi Nadi and hence its name, Bhrigu Nandi Nadi.

He spent lots of his time and resources collecting what was left of the original manuscripts of Bhrigu Nadi and Nandi Nadi from various locations. He translated them himself to study all the possible methods used in examining a birth chart.

Bhrigu Nadi is written by Maharishi Bhrigu, one of the seven sages or Saptarishis thousands of years ago. The origin of Nandi Nadi is not clear as of now; according to some, the author of Nandi Nadi is Nandi, the mount of Lord Shiva and depicted as a bull in Hindu mythology.

How Nadi Astrology differs from the existing form of Astrology?

Nadi Astrology is different from the currently popular form of Astrology in many ways. Nadi Astrology gives primary importance to the causatives or karakatwas of planets. Unlike Parashara's version of Astrology, Nadi Astrology does not assign much importance to the ascendant, Dasha Bhukthi, Ashtakavarga, etc. The persona and physical characteristics of a native are studied from the placement of Jupiter if the chart belongs to a male and Venus if it's a female birth chart; this is usually done from the ascendant in Vedic astrology.

In Nadi Astrology, transits and progression of the planets are given more importance, and Dasha Bhukthi is not considered for the timing of events. A wise astrologer can patently predict the likelihood of an event by scrutinizing the planetary progressions and transits alone with utmost accuracy.

Each planet is given certain karakatwas; one can predict matters associated with that planet by carefully analyzing its sign placement, aspects received from other planets, and conjunctions with other planets.

CAUSATIVES OR KARAKATWAS OF PLANETS

SUN

Atma (soul), name and fame, majestic, success, promotion, Government, higher posts, politics, dignity, authority, influential background, father, son, king, diplomacy, fiery nature, proud, male, royalty, pride, prestige, bile, right eye, heart, bones, fever, medicine & sociology, Sanskrit and its allied languages, circle shape, Kashyapa gotra, the state capital, gold and copper, spicy taste, ruby, wheat, Lord Shiva, status, radiant, eminent personalities, qualities of the trinity (Brahma, Vishnu & Maheswara), Tejo tattva, Sattvik, east, male progeny.

MOON

Mind, emotions, blame, thief, change, movement and travels, fraud, adultery, cunning, loss, fickle-minded, erratic, inconsistent, female progeny, beautiful eyes, Kapha/Vata, soft in speech, water, Tamo guna, divine, eloping, distraction, cheating, liquid, food, water, sell, loss, northwest, eyes, cold, cough, venereal, mental illness, lungs, epilepsy, infections, blood impurities, imagination, astrology, salt, food, dairy products, agriculture, animal feeding, chemicals, edible oils, mother, mother-in-law, aunt, queen, transfers, losses, Dravidian languages, square, Atreya gotra, Goddess Parvathy, inspiring & watery places like rivers, lakes, tank, silver, salt, drumstick, milk oozing trees, sweets, silk cloth, pearl, rice, arts, psychology, chemistry, hotel management.

MARS

Ego, passion, enmity, cruelness, dominating, quarrel, hazards, anger, stubbornness, pride, obstruct, power (shakti), electricity, manliness, haste, commander, bridge of the nose, hills, mountains, rocks, mines, metals, complex substances, hard metals, spheres, brother, husband, warrior, soldier, south direction, male progeny, Agni tattva, male, technical, machinery, realtors, sports, defense, mining, breaks, quarreling, harass, bile, cuts and wounds, muscle, teeth fire, spine, fire, accidents, mantra (powered languages), blood defects, yantra vidya, triangle, Bharadwaj gotra, red color, spicy, coral, red gram, Lord Subramanya, engineering, physics, mining, irrigation, sharp instruments hunting, fire, thorny trees, industries related to fire, electrical, mechanical, metal, mining, mineral, stone crushing, granite, arms, and ammunition.

MERCURY

Logic, romantic, friend, analytical, intelligence, education, diplomatic, logical, romantic, witty, sharing, intellect, learning, speech, commerce, business, accounting, publicity, media, teaching, astrology, publishing, gardening, brokerage, communication, power of judgment, writing, maternal uncle, wise persons, young, sister/brother, friend (male or female), lover, maternal uncle, counseling, forehead, skin, lungs, shoulders, skin-related ailments, lands, agro lands, creepers, education places, north direction, cipher, logical and encrypted languages, arrow, Atreya gotra, informative, bitter taste, Achyranthes Aspera, emerald, green gram, prince, Vishnu, Mathematics, statistics, green color, soft and attraction.

JUPITER

Noble, priestly, preacher, guide, master, religious, respect, honor, benevolent, wisdom, generous, successful, self-efforts, good works, liver, hernia, jaundice, fat, gas, acidity, Vata, obesity, yellow color, legal, advisory, endowments, temples, finance, prosperity, growth, northeast direction, akasha tattva, male progeny, Jeeva karaka, audit and accounts, philosophy, Lord Dakshina Murthy, Minister, chickpea, Yellow sapphire, papal tree, sweet, human development and research, Angiras gotra, rectangle shape, ancient languages, Kapha, sattva guna, coconut trees, sugarcane, betel nut, Vedas, interior wood decoration, elephants, prayers, devotional songs, mantras, charitable institutions, charities, jobs connected to the religions, advisory, legal, education department, life insurance department, meditation, healing, and religious preaching.

VENUS

Love, beauty, luxurious, prosperity, wealth, expertise, marriage, artistic, bhogha (indulgence), high profile, profitable, romantic, female progeny, Jala tatwa, rajasic, pleasure loving, wife, female, daughter and daughter-in-law, minister, higher learning, house, vehicle, assets, comforts, south east direction, Vata, southeast, diseases, uterine, phlegm, diabetes, semen, womb, ovaries, sexual, marketing, finance, beauty, arts, clubs, hotels, pleasure places, lima beans, white color, vitality, jasmine, artistic houses, cosmetic items, vanity bag, luxury cars, trees of watery places, honey bees, sour fruits, lotus, oval shape, master of demons, power of sanjeevini, expertise in literary languages, pentagonal shape, Bhargava gothra, places of wealth, joy and pleasures, sour taste, fig tree, diamond, beans, minister, goddess Lakshmi, housekeeping, jobs linked to banks and finance, performing arts, vehicle, luxury, entertainment, beauty parlors, visual media, music and women related fields.

SATURN

Servitude, stubbornness, karma, slow-progress, delay, lazy, works, business, promotion, work minded, blue color, physical disabilities, tobacco, factory, laborers, workers, last rites, Iswara, slow, sincere worker, Vayu tattva, west direction, Tamas, profession, low profiles, old materials, indigestion, rheumatism, karma karaka, labor, nerves, joints, gas, dark color, deep eyes, downward looks, cruel, blue sapphire, blue lilies, locomotive, application languages like blueprints, symbols, Kashyapa gotra, Lord Yama, industrial development places, iron, cold taste, Shami tree, sesame, servant, subjects like departmental and work-related training.

RAHU

Kalapurusha, injurious, last rites, shadow, unethical, laborious, low profile, illusions, dangers, other caste, foreign, ill health, danger, wheel, paternal grandfather, smugglers, deceivers, thieves, foreigners, drivers, obstructive, stammering, Vayu tatwa, tamasic, eccentric, pervert, addictions, secretive, intestine diseases, ear, cataract, poisons, pains, sick, big roads, huge grounds, half constructed or destroyed building, widespread trees, big manhole pipes, public transport vehicles, train, air plane, squint eyes, black magic, south west direction, vertical or reverse reading languages, wheel shaped, petrol, desert like places, amusement places, lead, astringent taste, durva grass, agate, black gram, low class people, goddess Chamundeswari, indicates subjects like chemicals, nuclear physics, foreign related topics, jobs related to foreign associated companies, secret dealings, atomic energy, air related, poisons, chemical industries, intoxicants, explosives, vehicle related, menial works, secondhand goods trade, black magic and witch craft.

KETU

Philosophy, bondage, aimless, end of karma, religious, ritualistic, moksha, diseases, disputable, ill-health, quitting, Moksha, grandfather, holy person, monks, philosopher, bondage, sanyasis, Agni tattva, Tamasic, spiritual, deject, divorce, unworldly, argumentative, law, medicine, occult, bondage, block, delink, abortive, pains/cuts, tumours, skin, private parts, constipation, piles, pitta, Lord Ganapathi, small, narrow, tail like things, obstructing places and passages, small dogs, rats, insects, arresting, hand cuffs, funeral, grey color, tailoring shops, tailors, materials, edges and ending, dried grass, rope, thread, hair, herbs/roots, loin cloth, trunk of elephant, banyan tree, tail portion of serpent, wire, wireless, north east direction, flag shape, Jaimini gotra, historic places, pilgrims, religious places, rusted metals, stale taste, salt reed-grass, cat's eye, horse gram, saints, seers, subjects like theology, medicine, law, astrology, jobs related to handicrafts, low paid, tailoring, weaving, spinning mills, healing and medicine, argumentative, wire, rope and pipe, alternative therapy.

CLASSIFICATION OF ZODIAC

In Nadi Astrology, Zodiacs or Rashis are categorized into four groups based on their direction:

East - Aries, Leo, Sagittarius

West - Gemini, Libra, Aquarius

North - Cancer, Scorpio, Pisces

South - Taurus, Virgo, Capricorn

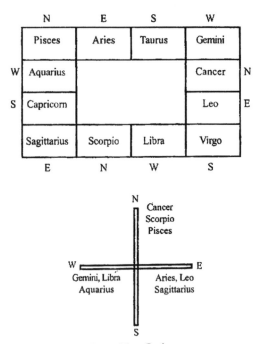

Based on the direction each sign represents, they are grouped into four categories, that is, Dharma, Artha, Kama and Moksha.

Dharma, Artha, Kama, and Moksha represent the four primary goals in human life. When analyzing a birth chart, we should arrange the planets according to their direction in the above-given format. Directions of planets are essential as it helps us to ascertain the functioning nature of planets and quickly intuit planetary aspects. From the positioning of the planets in the birth chart, one could easily predict an individual's primary motivation.

For example, consider a male chart where Jupiter, the Jeeva Karaka, is placed in Capricorn. Capricorn is a sign that comes under Saturn's lordship (Ishwaramsa). First of all, Capricorn signifies 'Kama,' which means that the thrust of the individual is to satisfy his desires. Capricorn is Ishwaramsa, so we can also say that he deceives himself with false pride and suffers from a superiority complex.

Likewise, we can predict results by looking at a planet and its sign placement. However, we should never predict anything blindly; you have to consider more important things like aspects, retrogression, parivartana yogas, if any, before reaching a conclusion.

If more planets or powerful planets are situated in a particular sign, then the motivation for that specific goal will be decisive. For example, suppose someone has three or more planets, including Jeeva Karaka Jupiter in Moksha Signs, and the rest of the planets are distributed into the other three directions. In that case, we can say that the native is peace-minded, religious, and a seeker of truth and salvation

PLANETARY ASPECTS IN NADI ASTROLOGY

In Nadi Astrology, general planetary aspects are not considered. While analyzing planetary aspects, we should first consider the planets in 1st, 2nd, 3rd, 7th, 5th, 9th, 11th, and 12th from the planet in question. Planets in 1st, 5th, and 9th are to be considered as if they are in conjunction, and planets in 3rd, 7th, and 11th from the planet in question should be regarded as the planets in opposition. We can safely ignore the planets in the 3rd and 11th houses if a planet is present in the 7th house because they are not exactly opposite to the planet in question, just in the opposite direction.

Planets in 2nd and 12th from the planet in question are essential because they are the planets in the succeeding and preceding signs and hence, must be given due importance while making predictions.

For example, suppose we are to analyze the educational prospects of a person. We should first consider Vidhya Karaka Mercury, and let's say Mars is situated in the 2nd house in the succeeding sign to Mercury. This configuration suggests that the native may study technical subjects; however, being an inimical planet to Mercury, Mars will create obstacles in his educational pursuits. In the same case, if Sun is situated in the 12th house, Sun will push Mercury to complete his education, and despite the obstacles, the native will do so; the same can be said if Sun is placed along with Mercury. However, if Sun is placed in the 2nd house and Mars, the whole picture changes. Being a friendly planet, Sun would empower Mars, which would only make it hard for the native to complete his education on time. Hence, the planets present in the preceding and succeeding signs must be emphasized.

There are a whole lot of things to consider before we could make predictions about education, career, or any other life aspects for that matter; the above-given example is purely hypothetical.

How do Retrograde and Debilitated Planets confer results?

Nadi Astrology gives great importance to the Retrogression and Debilitation of the planet. Planets always move clockwise, starting from Aries, Taurus, Gemini, etc. As seen from Earth, retrograde planets appear to move in an anticlockwise motion, as if they are going back to the preceding sign; essentially, they are looking back. Retrograde planets always aspect the rear sign only by half strength. This rule is only applicable to Mars, Mercury, Jupiter, Venus, and Saturn. Rahu and Ketu always move in an anticlockwise motion, and hence, this rule does not apply to them. Sun and Moon are never retrograde and are therefore exempted from this rule.

Debilitation of planets may not be necessarily malefic because a planet is constantly moving. You should keep in mind that a planet in its debilitation sign that will soon enter the following sign will be more potent than a planet nearing its debilitation sign from the previous sign. This situation can be compared to a person recovering after an accident and another person who will meet with an accident soon.

Debilitation of a planet is canceled to a certain extent if the planet in question is involved in a sign exchange with the its dispositor or more commonly known as Parivartana Yoga. In such cases, despite the initial sufferings in matters signified by that planet, he will gradually recover from the adverse effects.

Yogas and Doshas in Nadi Astrology

Parivartana Yoga

Parivartana Yoga is very important in astrology, and people having such yogas may experience sudden changes in their lives. This type of yoga can bring a person from rags to riches or from riches to rags. All these depend upon the potential of yoga and, most importantly, the planets involved.

Kuja Dosha

Kuja Dosha is widely regarded as an inauspicious yoga. Kuja Dosha is predicted in Nadi Astrology if Mars is afflicted by Ketu. Mars is the causative planet of marriage in any birth chart irrespective of gender, and Ketu signifies obstacles, end, Moksha etc. So, a combination of Mars and Ketu may create obstacles in getting married or may completely deny married life. This is especially true if they are in conjunction or in the same direction without any beneficial aspects.

Guru Karma Moksha Yoga

If Jupiter, Saturn, and Ketu are in conjunction or in successive signs or in the same direction, then this yoga will operate. This yoga can make one a teacher, doctor, or a highly reputed person in the society at the same time it may also create problems in work sphere and domestic life. This is a highly favorable combination for spiritual life. If Jupiter is not involved in the combination, it will create a lot of stress and problems in the work sphere, and he may probably settle late in life, without a favorable aspect from another planet. The aspect of Mars in the combination of

Saturn and Ketu is also considered as unfortunate for Professional as well as married life.

Dhoortha Karma Yoga

If Saturn, Mercury, and Rahu are in conjunction or in successive signs or in the same direction, then this yoga will operate. This yoga can make a person lazy and with little or no education. Aspects of benefic planets may cancel some bad effects of this yoga to a certain extent.

Guru Gangadhara Yoga

If Saturn, Jupiter and Moon are in conjunction or in successive signs or in the same direction, then this yoga will be Jupiter. The person born with this yoga will be very pious. He will acquire anything easily in life and will have a high reputation in society. He may become a teacher, a guide or a renowned preceptor. He will be having interested in studying psychology.

Raja Yoga

If Saturn, Sun and Jupiter are in conjunction or successive signs or the same direction, then this yoga will operate. He is from a well-reputed family; his father is a very prestigious person in society. He may be a politician or a government servant. He is very beautiful and attractive, and he will also acquire a name and fame in two society like his father. These are some of the crucial yogas mentioned; there are many other yogas. The potential results of a planetary combination can be ascertained by anyone just by correctly attributing the Karakatwas of planets. You have to keep in mind that a combination of friendly planets will always produce good results related to the affairs of the planets involved, and a combination of inimical planets will only result in adverse effects unless a benefic aspect is received.

FRIENDSHIP AND ENMITY BETWEEN PLANETS

None of the planets are inimical to each other. In astrology, planets are considered to be friendly, neutral, and inimical to each other based on the inherent qualities of planets.

SUN

Saturn is Tamo guna, whereas the Sun is for Rajo guna, so they are inimical to each other because of their inherent qualities. Sun is the causative planet for Soul or Atma. The soul is not interested in luxury or any other things that Venus represents because the soul aims to get salvation. So Venus is astrologically inimical to Sun. Rahu is a shadowy planet; it temporarily swallows the Sun causing Solar Eclipse. So astrologically, Rahu is considered to be an enemy of the Sun. Thus Sun is astrologically inimical to Venus, Saturn, and Rahu. He is neutral to Moon and friendly to the rest of the planets.

MOON

Moon is the causative planet of the mind, water, mother-in-law, divinity, etc. Rahu represents smoke and clouds and is inimical to Moon because clouds can cover up the Moon and make it appear dim.. If Rahu covers up the Moon, which is the causative planet of the mind, the native's mind may become foggy and eclipsed. Rahu also represents illusions or Maya. Venus and Moon are at odds with each other because Moon signifies expenditure, while Venus denotes wealth and hence are not concordant in their aspects. Thus Moon is inimical to Rahu and Venus, neutral to Sun, and the rest of the planets are her friends.

MARS

Mars is the causative planet of ego. Saturn represents a workman. One cannot work under someone with a strong ego and hence, Saturn and Mars are considered enemies. Rahu is Tamo guna, and Mars is Rajo Guna, so they are considered enemies. Mercury is intellect, and Mars is ego, so they are also considered enemies. Hence, Mars is not concordant with Saturn, Rahu, and Mercury. He is friendly with the rest of the planets.

MERCURY

Mercury is the planet of intellect; he dislikes egoistic Mars because of his "act first, think later" approach. So, Mercury and Mars are enemies. Similarly, Mercury is young, and it has no inclination towards salvation and is therefore not interested in things Ketu has to offer. Therefore, Mercury is inimical to Mars and Ketu and friendly to the other planets.

JUPITER

As per Nadi Astrology, Jupiter is not inimical to any other planets except that he sometimes acts as a neutral to Moon and Rahu. That's why Jupiter is called the most beneficial planet in any birth chart.

VENUS

Venus is friendly with Saturn, Mars, Mercury, and Rahu and neutral to Ketu and Jupiter. She is inimical to Moon and Sun.

SATURN

Sun, Moon, Mars, and Rahu are his enemies. The rest of the planets are his friends.

RAHU

Rahu is friendly with all other planets except Sun, Moon, and Mars.

KETU

Ketu is inimical to Mercury and Saturn. He is neutral to Sun and Moon and friendly with the other planets. Saturn is sometimes considered his friend.

These are the key points to keep in mind while analyzing a birth chart. Not only planets, the signs in which they are placed must also be given due importance while predicting results.

Two Planetary Combinations

Planetary Combinations are formed by the association of a certain number of planets through their placements, aspects and conjunctions. Here, the results of two planetary combinations of all planets are given. Planetary Combinations should only be considered if they are in the same direction (trines), conjunction, successive signs, or in opposition.

SUN WITH MOON

Sun, the governing planet for father with Moon indicates that the native's father may have to travel over many places or the native may settle in a different place away from his home.

SUN WITH MARS

The father of the native may be highly self-assertive and egoistic, and he is quick-tempered and will have supportive brothers. In a female chart, Mars signifies husband, which means that her husband is powerful with a good reputation but short-tempered.

SUN WITH MERCURY

The native's father is intelligent, knowledgeable, and has an honorable status in society. He is business-minded. The native himself will also be an intelligent man and given to enjoying sensual pleasures.

SUN WITH JUPITER

This is the combination of Soul and Life, which indicates that the native has special skills and knowledge and ever strives to attain honor and prestige in society and his efforts will be crowned with success. He will shine as an outstanding figure in society being respected by politicians and people in authority. His father might also be given to divine contemplation, enjoying honor and prestige in the society, and well versed in many fields.

SUN WITH VENUS

The native earns money through, royal patronage and organizations dealing in luxury goods. This may indicate that he is not lucky in having a male progeny or his wife may have a miscarriage. His wife hoards valuable ornaments and jewelers.

SUN WITH SATURN

The native's father may have come up in life with difficulty. He may follow the same profession as his father. Though the native and his father are together in the family, now and again there will be misunderstandings between them.

SUN WITH RAHU

If Sun is with Rahu, the representative of the eternal time factor, such a native's father will have to face and overcome accidental death. He will get male progeny after a lot of difficulties.

SUN WITH KETU

The native's father will have to face many hurdles before earning a name and fame. He may be well versed in divine contemplation and metaphysics. He likes agriculture and rural residence. The native's children attain name and fame and may work in government organizations.

MOON WITH MARS

The native's brother may have traveled to many places or he will reside with his relatives. His mother may have to face danger from fire. He is fickle-minded.

MOON WITH MERCURY

A person having this planetary combination will be highly intelligent. He has an intuitive knack and can know well in advance what is going to happen in the future. Such a person will not strive hard to study but scores maximum marks in every subject he studies in his class. He will be well versed in several fields of knowledge and has many friends to give company to him.

MOON WITH JUPITER

The native may settle in a place away from his native place. His mother may be engaged in divine contemplation and will be known for her pious nature.

MOON WITH VENUS

He will have a suspicious mentality and his mother may have come up in life with difficulty. She will accumulate wealth and jewelry. His wife may hail from a family outside the circle of his relatives and friends.

MOON WITH SATURN

The profession of the native may involve constant traveling. His mother may suffer from phlegm and windy complaints. He will be a spendthrift.

MOON WITH RAHU

The native may suffer from fright, delusion, and the effects of witchcraft. There will be a water body near his residence. He may suffer from mental illness or perturbations.

MOON WITH KETU

The native's Mother is of helping mentality and helps poor and needy people. Even though she is not well educated she is well versed in spirituality and she may suffer from cold and windy complaints. The native may think about renunciation at some point in life.

MARS WITH MERCURY

He may have quarrels with his brother frequently. He may face obstacles in his educational pursuits. The native may get deceived by the opposite sex.

MARS WITH JUPITER

The native is good at heart. He may have an elder brother. He suffers from blood pressure and is short-tempered. He is highly emotional and feels a sense of superiority over others.

MARS WITH VENUS

He will have brothers. He may learn some secrets of art. His brother earns well and hoards money, leading a life of utter luxury. His married life will be above satisfactory.

MARS WITH SATURN

This combination indicates that one of his brothers will have to face many difficulties and enemies. In whatever

The field of the profession he engages himself will be relating to machinery and its management. He may change many professions and still, there will be constant hurdles in his professional field.

MARS WITH RAHU

The native is very emotional and he may get angry for even flimsy reasons. He may have to face and overcome dangers due to machinery and air transport. He may also suffer in family life on account of mutual suspicion and misunderstanding. The native will be subject to overconfidence and great mental excitement at certain times

MARS WITH KETU

The native is having Kuja dosha. He may suffer from nervous debility. He may marry with difficulty at a comparatively later age. Family disputes may arise after his marriage.

MERCURY WITH JUPITER

A native having of such a planetary combination in his birth chart is an intellectual. He may attain mastery over several branches of knowledge and becomes proficient in scholarship.

MERCURY WITH VENUS

The native is given to sweet talk and welcomes everybody with politeness and hearty greetings. He is dramatic in his manners and appears extremely polite. He adopts several means and sees to it that he gains his object somehow without causing trouble to others. He will achieve proficiency in several arts like music, playing over the flute, etc. They enjoy honor and prestige in society. Natives with such a planetary combination in their birth charts, whether male or female, somehow make friends with the members of the opposite sex without much difficulty.

MERCURY WITH SATURN

The native is intelligent. Though he is so he does not have the knack to exhibit the same outwardly and may appear as though he is dull. He is a bit lazy. He may get involved in transactions that do not smack of illegality or deceit. He is fortunate in land dealing and trade transactions.

MERCURY WITH RAHU

The native is intelligent but, may suffer several mental delusions. He gets on well in photography and camera techniques. He will be somewhat dull-witted.

MERCURY WITH KETU

The native is interested in divine contemplation and self-realization. He is intuitive and can attain scholarships without much effort in any field of knowledge. He may also lose his sense of hearing and is likely to get skin ailments. The native will be well versed in writing, drawing, etc.

JUPITER WITH VENUS

The native is interested in arguments and disputes and is well versed in several fields of knowledge. His wife is given to divine contemplation, philanthropic, quiet, bright, and magnetic in her appearance. The native earns money with divine grace or by the divine grace of his wife's personality.

JUPITER WITH SATURN

The two planets govern religion and profession respectively. The native will have a beautiful nose and cheeks and will desire only good things in life. In whatever field of profession, they will attain mastery over there. The native's words carry a lot of weight in society.

JUPITER WITH RAHU

The native is born in a famous place and will be having a good-looking and possess a round-shaped body. He may be estranged from his brother. He is well versed in several fields of knowledge, travels over many places. He may suffer from polio.

JUPITER WITH KETU

The native may have been born in a place that is either a place of pilgrimage or having a temple of a divine female deity. He will be well versed in Vedic literature. He is thoughtful, pious, and is not desirous of popularity. He is interested in divine contemplation. The native will always be given to a life of renunciation.

VENUS WITH SATURN

He will earn his livelihood by working in an organization dealing with financial management or in a business dealing with luxury goods. He will gain financially through trade transactions.

VENUS WITH RAHU

Venus is the Jeeva Karaka planet for females. This combination indicates that the native is born with a magnificent female origin. The native may have immense wealth and commands cars and motor cavalcade and will prosper in the film industry and secret trade deals.

VENUS WITH KETU

The native is given to divine contemplation. The native may enjoy abundance in luxurious clothes, fertile lands, and motor cars. But she will not be interested in sensual and worldly pleasures.

SATURN WITH RAHU

The native may earn his livelihood through either photography or working in a film unit. He may amass money secretly without the knowledge of the government.

SATURN WITH KETU

Whatever profession the native engages in, there will be a lot of hindrances to his progress. He will be interested in renouncing life altogether. He will have very little interest in worldly affairs and he will somehow pull on in life with absolutely no interest. There will be several hurdles for his progress in life. Such natives will somehow eke out their livelihood by doing odd jobs such as weaving, tailoring, printing, etc.

From the above-given combinations, you can see that all the results are stated only by giving importance to the Causative or Karakatwas of Planets. Similarly while analyzing a birth chart, one should give primary importance to Karakatwas and to the signs in which they are placed to accurately predict results.

GENERAL RESULTS OF PLANETS IN SIGNS

SUN IN ARIES

Sun is exalted in Aries and hence considered the zodiac's capital sign. A person born with Sun in Aries with beneficial planetary aspects will have an influential father enjoying patronage and help from the government. The native's sons would also be bestowed with such privileges and will achieve fame and name and work in technical fields.

SUN IN TAURUS

The natives having Sun placed in Gemini in their birth chart will have a financially well-to-do father. The sons of such natives are also likely to have their line of work related to financial administration.

SUN IN GEMINI

The native's father came up in life through his intelligence and brainpower. Both his father and son are known for their intelligence. The sons of the native will get on in life in a profession relating to art and commerce.

SUN IN CANCER

The native's father is a lover of art. His son will get on in life in a place other than his birthplace and will travel extensively during his lifetime.

SUN IN LEO

The native's father is stout, exercises authority over others, and enjoys prestige and favor of influential people in society. His talk is definite and to the point. The native's son is also like his grandfather enjoying royal patronage.

SUN IN VIRGO

The native's father is known for his intelligence, enjoying the help and cooperation of one and all. His son will also prosper among similar lines.

SUN IN LIBRA

His father has come up in life from grass root level in his later life. He gets on in life with financial management as his profession. His son also will prosper on similar lines.

SUN IN SCORPIO

The father of the native has come up in life after a hard struggle. He has his profession related to machinery or land dealings. His son also will get on in life by adopting a similar career.

SUN IN SAGITTARIUS

The father of the native is contemplative and philosophical in his outlook, having divine contemplation as his aim in life. In his profession, he will enjoy moderate success. The native's sons will get on in life honorably.

SUN IN CAPRICORN

The father of the native has come up in life slowly is given to occasional fits of anger and outbursts. The native is fond of traveling. His son follows the path of his grandfather and adopts a profession relating to travel and machinery.

SUN IN AQUARIUS

The father of such natives is known for their discretion. The native is intelligent and well-versed in occult subjects. He enjoys prestige in society, and so does his son.

SUN IN PISCES

The father of the native is honorable and given to divine contemplation. He is quite good-looking. His son also will be similar in life, enjoying favor and patronage of influential people in society.

MOON IN ARIES

When Moon, the planet signifying the mind and mother, is placed in Aries, the native will be stubborn, aggressive, and prone to violent outbursts. The native's mother, though she cannot help people going through difficulties, will at least sympathize with them.

MOON IN TAURUS

The native is broadminded and thinks that they are special in some way. The native's mother is influential in society, respected, and loved by most people. Despite all this, the native's mind resorts to thoughts of a low order at times.

MOON IN GEMINI

The native is intelligent, social, and resorts to logic to address any issues. He is quite faithful and engages in trade pursuits, and so does his mother.

MOON IN CANCER

The native is fickle-minded, philanthropic, and a lover of art. The native's mother is also similar in nature and popular.

MOON IN LEO

The person is assertive and straightforward while expressing his ideas. He strives to attain honor in life. His mother enjoys and exercises authority in the family.

MOON IN VIRGO

He is intelligent, mixes with the members of society, and engages himself in several social activities. He is attentive to minute details and usually makes decisions only after considering all the possible outcomes. He is discreet, and his mother is wise and tries to accumulate as much money as possible.

MOON IN LIBRA

This person has financial ambitions. Though outwardly protesting that he has no intentions to save money, he secretly tries to hoard as much money as possible. His mother also has the same capitalistic bent of mind, and she suffers from an overheated constitution and rheumatism.

MOON IN SCORPIO

This person is peculiar, trying to indulge in several matters of unproductive nature. He is fickle-minded. His mother will keep herself aloof from activities beneficial to society. If Moon does not receive any beneficial aspects, she may suffer public ridicule. The nature of such people is to instigate others and make them dance to their tunes. These people will have developed the art of preaching philosophy to others.

MOON IN SAGITTARIUS

This person has critical faculties, is broadminded, pious, and gets discouraged due to mental worries. His mother is god-fearing and come up in life despite numerous obstacles. She suffers from cold and allied complaints.

MOON IN CAPRICORN

He is highly emotional, makes hasty decisions, and suffers due to this. He will often ruminate over a single desire wishing to fulfill the same. His mother frequently suffers from the bad effects of heat and cold and ill health.

MOON IN AQUARIUS

He will always be engaged in secret mental manipulations, coming out with his revelations appropriately. His mother is good-looking, philanthropic, and suffers from rheumatic complaints.

MOON IN PISCES

He will possess shiny eyes and is well versed in metaphysical matters. He is romantic, somewhat fickle-minded, and helps others in times of need. His mother suffers from the bad effects of cold and is given to divine contemplation.

MARS IN ARIES

Mars rules Aries, it's also his Moolatrikona sign and the house of the exaltation of the royal planet Sun. This planet rules over machinery and anything that's mechanical in nature. Such natives are bright, quite efficient, and enjoys the friendship of influential people in society. He has a tall body, ruddy complexion, and is interested in making money from organizations dealing in machinery.

MARS IN TAURUS

This person is patient, interested in educational pursuits, is of an adjusting temperament, getting on well with others. He is lucky and is friendly with his kith and kin. He is of medium height and earns money with the least effort. He has a penchant for beautiful things. Further, this position indicates that the person will be well versed in the design and manufacture of aesthetically pleasing machine models. In a female horoscope, this indicates a good-natured husband.

MARS IN GEMINI

The native is intelligent and quite patient. He is afraid of rushing through in any field of profession. A member of his brother's family will have risen in life from scratch after undergoing several difficulties and hardships. If a female birth chart, this indicates that her husband is intelligent and hails from the West direction from her birth place, and is of medium height and good looking. In predicting about the husband's profession, it is stated that he adopts a career involving automation.

MARS IN CANCER

The native is of mild temperament, afraid, and in whatever field he enters, blames, accusations, etc., will be there to confront him. Further, he is given to loud talk but lacks courage. Such people are naturally afraid of their wives being henpecked in nature. Such persons will be taken in by deceitful people and deceived. He is fickle-minded. A member of his brother's family will have indulged in dishonorable pursuits and suffered great infamy as a consequence. If Mars is located in Cancer in a female horoscope, the husband is of a round face, dark complexion, hailing from East, and residing in the north direction. He is of tall build and suffers from anemia and debility now and then. But if Mars is subject to the aspect of benefic planets, it indicates promising results. The husband will be in a profession full of travel, and he earns through an agency dealing in liquids and chemicals.

MARS IN LEO

The native is arrogant, proud, and stubborn. He expects everyone else to respect him. He has a beautiful body. A member of his brother's family will be quite influential in royal circles; if in a female horoscope the husband hails from the East and is in a profession in an organization having governmental support, is given to loud talk. He is likely to suffer ill-health due to bilious and overheated constitution.

MARS IN VIRGO

The native is mild tongued and will abhor egoism and arrogance. His brother earns money quite easily by making use of his intelligence. He suffers from nervous debility, over-heat, and skin ailments. In a female chart, this indicates that the husband hails from the East and resides in the southern direction, is of medium height, stout build, intelligent, and of mediocre fortune.

MARS IN LIBRA

The native is mad after money, quite faithful and trustworthy. He will grab any opportunities to earn money if its within his reach. His brother will also get on well in life. He will have his profession in an organization having financial transactions and account matters or where luxury articles are dealt with. The native's brother will have a bright future in a career connected with luxury articles. He should guard against the consumption of sour and spicy food items. If a female horoscope, the husband is of medium height given to sweet talk, resides in the Western direction, and is quite fortunate.

MARS IN SCORPIO

The native is stubborn, bides his time for giving trouble, and gives trouble to others with a smile in his face. He is self-centered and may suffer from blood defects. His brother is somewhat dull and travels over many places. He avoids divine contemplation.

MARS IN SAGITTARIUS

The native has critical faculties, somewhat given to divine contemplation, though loud-mouthed, possesses a kind-hearted nature. His brother also has the same characteristics and qualities. In a female horoscope, the husband hails from the East, is tall, honest, intelligent, and attains great fame and name after his marriage. He will have a happy family life. He has to guard against the bad effects of cold and rheumatism.

MARS IN CAPRICORN

The native is self-assertive and tries to stick to his opinions at any cost. He speaks harshly without heeding to the consequences. He does well to one and all going out of his way to oblige them and gets only blames and abuses in return. Whatever he does, whether good or bad, attracts the ire of his enemies, who will always be plotting against him. Though he loves his wife very much, his wife will often wish to be rid of his company. At times he behaves as though only he and nobody else matters in the world. One of his brother's family members is in a prestigious profession. In a female horoscope, the husband hails from the South and is quite powerful and influential with a ruddy complexion, though lean, tall, short-tempered, and stubborn. Now and then, there will be misunderstandings between him and his mother-in-law. He has to guard against heart complaints and biliousness.

MARS IN AQUARIUS

In a female horoscope, the husband hails from the West, of a round face, quite respectable, and has great respect for his elders and preceptors. The native appears to be mild when circumstances demand so, however, he asserts himself and may seem harsh if things are not going his way. He is liked by others and suffers from an overheated constitution. He need not have to face any special difficulties in his family life.

MARS IN PISCES

The native is given to divine contemplation. Though not much, he is provided to help others and is somewhat pious. In a female horoscope, the husband hails from the north, is tall, and recites Vedic mantras. He has immense faith in his family members and progeny. Mars is the planet governing brothers, husband, fire, enemies. Although Mars controls the ego element in men, he will bring about breaks and disturbances in the native's professional career every now and then..

MERCURY IN ARIES

The native is well versed in the mechanical work, always engaged but somewhat stubborn.

MERCURY IN TAURUS

He is an affectionate moneyed man and a good conversationalist. He is knowledgeable in occult matters.

MERCURY IN GEMINI

He is known for his brains. In authorship and trade matters, he earns name and fame in the society and is know for his sharp wit.

MERCURY IN CANCER

Though he is well educated, he has to face many impediments in life. He is known for his fickle nature as also suspicious mentality. He gets a bad name on account of women and friends. He has an interest in art and artistic pursuits.

MERCURY IN LEO

He tries to get the patronage of influential persons in society. He gets possession of his land. He has only one younger brother. He gets governmental support.

MERCURY IN VIRGO

He is extremely intelligent, gets interested in commercial transactions, and achieves good companions' friendship when only Mercury is in Virgo; he gets the help of a lady companion. He has got a lot of clout in society.

MERCURY IN LIBRA

He has got a knack for managing financial affairs. By this, he earns money, lands, house, etc.

MERCURY IN SCORPIO

There will be a lot of impediments to his educational career. There is some sort of mental delusion coming in the way of prosecuting his studies and diligence. Despite his reasonable intellect, he has to overcome many hurdles to come up in life. If he has a younger brother, he will likely get on in life through the agency of machinery and hard labor.

MERCURY IN SAGITTARIUS

He is intelligent, given to divine contemplation, and a sort of lonely voyager in the high seas of life. His last younger brother is philanthropic and given to religious thinking.

MERCURY IN CAPRICORN

Though good-natured and tolerating in communication, he is ruled by somebody else. To complete his educational career, he has to undergo many difficulties and face many critical situations and harassment from others. But there is this saving grace that his younger brother helps him to overcome all these with his expert knowledge of machinery and vehicles.

MERCURY IN AQUARIUS

He is slow, good-natured, and tries to understand things. But it takes a long time for him to do all this. He is very economical with words and tries to answer a hundred queries with only one term as a reply. His brother behaves at first as though he is quite ignorant and then gradually comes up in life.

MERCURY IN PISCES

Though he completes his educational career slowly, he is given divine contemplation. He has the desire to visit holy pilgrimage places. He enjoys prestige in society. If he has a brother, he will be of modest educational attainments.

JUPITER IN ARIES

He has a tall body stature, a small nose, and is always engaged in work and business affairs. He suffers from bilious complaints.

JUPITER IN TAURUS

He is of medium height and is given to a life of comfort and luxury. He likes hardworking people. Health-wise, he suffers from gastric troubles.

JUPITER IN GEMINI

He is intelligent, affectionate, mixes freely with one and all. He earns sufficient wealth property and is of medium height.

JUPITER IN CANCER

He has got a semi-crescent-shaped nose. The heart line extends in the area below the three fingers in his hand. He has a beautifully shaped body, is somewhat stout, and attracts everyone. This power of attraction lies in the shape of his nose. The native having Jupiter in Cancer will have one of his subsidiary professions as either art or medicine. He suffers from throat ailments and the ill effects of cold. If one attentively listens to what he says, one will be surprised to realize many of his casual utterances are coming true. Though he appears to be a person of no consequence in his younger days, later on in life, he assumes a position of honor and prestige of considerable magnitude in society.

JUPITER IN LEO

He has a nose resembling that of the kits, a slender waist, given to loud talk, and enjoys the cooperation and patronage of influential and elderly persons in society. He suffers from nervous debility and bilious complaints.

JUPITER IN VIRGO

He is of medium height, intelligent, and achieves his desires through careful planning. Though slight in build, he is good-looking, despite a snub nose. His health will also be good.

JUPITER IN LIBRA

He is of medium height, fond of good food and women. He is pleasure-loving. He is ever interested in accumulating wealth and guarding his honor and prestige.

JUPITER IN SCORPIO

He has an asymmetrically shaped body, dark red complexion, and medium height and is interested in hard tasks. He is narrow-minded and suffers from the evil effects of poisonous materials, overheat and bilious complaints. He cannot easily vent what he has inside his mind.

JUPITER IN SAGITTARIUS

He has a long nose, is garrulous, suffers from bad effects of cold, is affectionate, and gains his ends through righteous ways.

JUPITER IN CAPRICORN

He is stout and attractive but often suffers from ill-health due to the bad effects of wind and cold and, general weakness. He has a wide nose and does not enjoy the favor and affection of his kith and kin and outsiders. Even in his pursuit of pleasure, he has to face several difficulties.

JUPITER IN AQUARIUS

He is of medium height and round in build. He tries to understand philosophy by constant experimentation. He fiercely guards his honor and prestige. Whichever field he enters, he desires to establish his hegemony. He suffers from gastric complaints.

JUPITER IN PISCES

He is tall in stature and attractive. He is an intellectual and earns status and prestige in society. He is interested in Vedic literature and divine contemplation. He suffers from excessive perspiration.

VENUS IN ARIES

The wife of a native born with Venus in Aries in his birth chart hails from a decent family. She is somewhat tall, having a triangular face. She is courageous. She prospers and acquires lands after marriage. The native with this placement earns well in a profession connected with machinery and organizations of the central government. With the least effort, he yields maximum gain.

VENUS IN TAURUS

He gets monetary gains through financial transactions, accounts maintenance, and trade. His wife is somewhat tall, has good-looking facial features, and is intelligent. His sisters and mother-in-law exhibit their prestige and prowess whenever they visit his house. The female progeny born to him will be of mediocre fortunes. His sisters will be well off in life.

VENUS IN GEMINI

The native of the horoscope, having Venus in such a position, gains money through trade. His wife is intelligent and interested in sensual pleasures. She is affectionate towards her kith and kin. She has a protruding face and is of medium height. She earns and spends well. His sisters and daughters will be known for their rational nature.

VENUS IN CANCER

He achieves monetary gains through art, fluids, and travel, and his income will be dependable. That is, he has to travel extensively to earn money. He marries a wife outside his relative's circle. She will be quite good-looking and artistic in temperament. Her moods will sometimes be conflicting. Added to all this, she suffers from ill-health and is likely to get a bad name. There will be several impediments to the general welfare of his sisters and daughters. Irrespective of his large earnings, he will be known for his polite manners. He has got flat-shaped cheeks, almost concave in appearance. He has earned the ability and knack of enjoying sensual pleasures outside the bonds of wedlock. The general trend is that his family's happiness is the minimum.

VENUS IN LEO

He derives financial gains through royal patronage or by the cooperation and help of the government. His wife hails from a prestigious family and is very strict in her conduct. She is highly egoistic and hoards gold and jewelry. She has an overheated constitution. His sisters are also similar. His wife has something magnetic about her, and his daughter marries a person from a prestigious family.

VENUS IN VIRGO

His sisters will have to face and overcome many hurdles and difficulties in life, including a damaged reputation. They are good conversationalists. His wife is talkative and blameworthy. He does not believe his wife many a time. His wife is of medium height, not very short in stature. She is calculative and of medium good looks. The native gains financially through trade and commercial transactions. His wife somehow accumulates and hoards a considerable amount of money, straining her every nerve to do so.

VENUS IN LIBRA

Women belonging to the native's family are quite fortunate in life; though his wife is discreet in her behavior, she is somewhat hasty in her talk. If she minds, she can mean and do well to others but indulges in arrogant behavior. However, she sees that the family is happy and contented with herself as the housewife. He builds his own house and derives financial gains.

VENUS IN SCORPIO

His wife is somewhat ruddy in complexion and tallish in build. She is known for her courageous and enterprising nature, almost bordering on stubbornness. She will not be so cooperative with her father-in-law. Even with her kith and kin, she will be somewhat irritable. The native gains through land dealings and machinery. His wife, though lean-bodied, is quite strong but suffers from blood defects and a bilious constitution.

VENUS IN SAGITTARIUS

The native will be tall, having luxurious tresses of hair if a female. Her facial features will be quite attractive, and despite her high educational attainments, she will be modest and well-mannered. The sisters of the native, if male, will be intelligent and educated. The native earns well by adopting decent means. The native's wife suffers from the ill effects of cold.

VENUS IN CAPRICORN

His wife is of darkish ruddy complexion, cold constitution, quite good looking with broad facial features. She suffers from the ill effects of cold and wind. However, no matter how much he earns, everything will be spent with no scope for any saving. Although the native's wife is constantly unwell, he will be quite affectionate. The native's sisters and daughters are good-looking, and his wife will have attractive facial features. He derives financial benefits through fluids, art, and machinery.

VENUS IN AQUARIUS

The native's wife has a round face of medium height and though slow in her talk, talks quite meaningfully. She is darkish red in complexion and gradually attains a good status in life. His sisters will get on in life with financial stability. The native gains financially within two years of his marriage. His wife will suffer from phlegm-related ailments and vomiting, and cold complaints.

VENUS IN PISCES

His wife will have a narrow face and will be good-looking. She will be known for her patience and sterling qualities of both head and heart. Even supposing his wife does not command good looks, fortune smiles upon her and bestows prosperity wherever she sets foot in. His sisters would also get on in life without facing many difficulties. The native having Venus in Pisces in his birth chart will have fish-shaped cheeks. He is wealthy and leads a luxurious life. Though some people with this placement are known to have had ordinary-looking wives, they will especially be fortunate in life.

SATURN IN ARIES

The native reaps his fortune through the instrumentality of Mars, the governing planet for powerful machinery. In his palm, the line of fortune develops slowly. There is every likelihood of getting cooperation and patronage of the Central Government.

SATURN IN TAURUS

The native-born with Saturn in the house of Venus, the governing planet for wealth, will prosper in his career and gradually attains financial stability. He will continue in the profession of luxury goods, entertainment, or financial institutions.

SATURN IN GEMINI

The native has a profession connected with commercial trade and accounts matters and earns well by sheer dint of his intelligence.

SATURN IN CANCER

This zodiac house has a connection with art, fluids, motion, and water and will have the native's profession relating to these. He is liable to be deceived by others, or failing this; he will have falsehoods dominating his transactions;

SATURN IN LEO

The native will have his profession under the government or a prestigious organization. One of his elder brothers will be the court favorite or enjoying royal favor.

SATURN IN VIRGO

He will have a profession relating to trade and commerce. He will earn well using his brains rather than brawns, and money comes easily.

SATURN IN LIBRA

He will prosper in an institution dealing with financial management, law, and luxury goods.

SATURN IN SCORPIO

He ekes out his livelihood with difficulty in an organization dealing with machinery, Engineering, Land management, mineral exploration, etc.

SATURN IN SAGITTARIUS

He has a pious and noble bent of mind and earns his bread without much effort. He is quite innovative and knows how to get things done.

SATURN IN CAPRICORN

He will work in career fields related to heavy machinery and power-oriented projects, failing which agriculture and fluid management. Capricorn is a sign of exertion, physical as well as mental.

SATURN IN AQUARIUS

He will be interested in occult subjects and quite knowledgeable too. There is a certain amount of eccentricity in their character.

SATURN IN PISCES

He will flourish in a profession connected to teaching, religion, spirituality, philosophy, etc. He will occupy a position of reverence and will be known for his noble nature.

These are general results of planets through each sign and are subject to modifications on other influencing factors like aspects, retrogression, planetary interchange, etc.

PRACTICAL EXAMPLES

Example 1 – Male Birth Chart

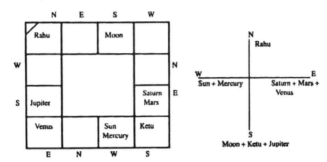

Let us study the vocation of the native from the given birth chart, which is seen from the placement of Saturn.

In the above-given chart, the planetary combination of Jupiter+Moon+Ketu indicates that he is a liberator of minds.

Jupiter – The Native

Moon – Mind

Ketu – Liberation

In the East direction, the royal sign, Leo is occupied by Saturn and Mars along with Venus posited in the same direction in Sagittarius, which is an auspicious combination due to the presence of Venus. The successive direction to Saturn is the combination of Jupiter+Moon+Ketu.

This suggests that the native may be a teacher due to the presence of Jupiter, Moon, and Ketu in 2nd to Saturn. Saturn's position in Leo and the presence of Sun in the opposite direction suggests that he occupy a position with considerable authority and may be working for a government institution. Mars and Venus in the same direction as Saturn suggest that the institution may be teaching related to machinery and he also earns well.

The above birth chart belongs to the Principal of a government-run Engineering College.

Likewise, predictions should be made by taking the causative planets, aspects received and signs involved.

Example 2 – Female Birth Chart

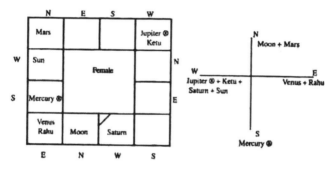

Let us study, the educational prospects of the person from the above birth chart. Education is studied from Mercury.

Mercury is posited in Capricorn alone but receives an aspect from Jupiter because he is retrograde, which ensures good educational prospects. Since Mercury is also retrograde, he looks on to the rear sign where Venus and Rahu are posited. Venus stands for gains and Rahu for huge, which means vast gains in education. So, she must be a well-educated person.

The native of the above birth chart is highly qualified and holds a Post Graduate Degree.

Example 3 – Male Birth Chart

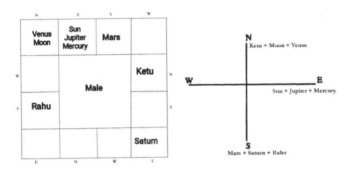

Let us study the prospects of marriage for this person. The causative planet for marriage irrespective of gender is Mars.

The combination of Mars+Saturn+Rahu is considered unfortunate because Saturn and Rahu are bitter enemies of Mars. So, he may be having some kind of disabilities in his limbs. This combination is opposed by the combination of Moon+Venus+Ketu, which is again a bad combination as both the female planets are under the clutches of Ketu.

Hence, there are no chances of getting married, despite being an affluent person (Sun+ Mercury+ Jupiter).

This person is unmarried, and he has a disability with one of his legs.

He is an respected person and earn handsomely. He is working in a factory in a considerably good post.

From the above examples, you must have understood that primary importance is always given to the karaka about that particular aspect of your life. It is always useful to convert planets in the above-given format to make predictions easy.

OM TAT SAT

Printed in Great Britain
by Amazon

22767931R00034